Isaac F. Tillinghast

A Manual of Vegetable Plants

Containing the experiences of the author in starting all those kinds of

vegetables which are most difficult for a novice to produce from seeds

Isaac F. Tillinghast

A Manual of Vegetable Plants
*Containing the experiences of the author in starting all those kinds of vegetables
which are most difficult for a novice to produce from seeds*

ISBN/EAN: 9783337363598

Printed in Europe, USA, Canada, Australia, Japan

Cover: Foto ©Andreas Hilbeck / pixelio.de

More available books at **www.hansebooks.com**

A MANUAL

OF

VEGETABLE PLANTS.

CONTAINING

THE EXPERIENCES OF THE AUTHOR IN STARTING ALL THOSE
KINDS OF VEGETABLES WHICH ARE MOST DIFFICULT
FOR A NOVICE TO PRODUCE FROM SEEDS.

WITH

THE BEST METHODS KNOWN FOR COMBATING AND REPELLING
NOXIOUS INSECTS, AND PREVENTING THE DISEASES
TO WHICH GARDEN VEGETABLES
ARE SUBJECT.

BY

ISAAC F. TILLINGHAST.

FACTORYVILLE, PA.:
TILLINGHAST BROTHERS.
—
1878.

S. W. Green,
Printer and Electrotyper,
16 & 18 Jacob Street,
New York.

PREFACE.

WE offer this little volume to the world, honestly believing that its perusal will benefit all its readers who are so situated as to apply its teachings to practice.

As a literary writer we claim no credit, and invite no criticism upon our work as a rhetorical essay, or in a literary point of view.

It has been written entirely during odd hours snatched from business pursuits, and its text must be very imperfect. In its composition we have endeavored to be as brief and concise as possible, knowing well that by the majority of people in this hurrying age the wheat will be considered more valuable without the chaff than with it. Ideas of value are wanted. We have endeavored to supply them.

If, after a careful perusal, the reader agrees with us in thinking that the knowledge herein contained is worth to him more than the price of the volume, he must rest abundantly satisfied with his investment.

We are aware that more printed paper may be obtained elsewhere for less money than in this instance.

But that argues nothing. Good milk may be obtained at a far less cost for a given quantity than cream or butter. We charge for the ideas, which are our own, and not for the paper on which they are printed, or the covers which contain them. The latter are easily obtainable, the former are not. If you buy a pound of sugar for a shilling, and the merchant sends it to you in a china bowl, you will thank him for the bowl rather than grumble because he did not send a ten-quart pail.

That all who purchase a copy of this work may be enabled to profit by its teachings, an hundred-fold upon their investment, is the sincere wish of

THE AUTHOR.

CONTENTS.

PART FIRST.

PART SECOND.

PART FIRST.

GROWING PLANTS UNDER GLASS.

In this broad and fair but fickle and undulating clime, where Dame Nature's promises of flowery spring-time are so frequently frowned upon by a polar wave, which drives the life-blood back to the very heart of every unprotected living thing, some kind of protection from the lingering wintry blasts is an absolute necessity to every grower of early garden vegetables, whether he be a producer of them in large quantities for market purposes, or only seeks to supply his own table with early delicacies, or his garden with plants which are to be the germs of future substantials. Some kind of protection from the cold above, and an addition to the natural warmth below the growing plants, is required; and to meet this end, the heat which is developed by the slow combustion of vegetable matter or the decomposition of stable manures has generally been the accepted means of accomplishing the desired object.

THE MANURE HOT-BED has been so frequently described, and the best manner of constructing it so fully dwelt upon by all the principal agricultural journals, works on gardening, and seed catalogues, which have been freely scattered over the land, that we deem a description of it altogether unnecessary in our present work, especially as we think that the day of using *manure for fuel* will soon be known only in the recollections of the past. The inestimable value which we, as tillers of the soil, long ago learned to put upon manure for plant food, and the cheapness with which the desired amount of heat could be produced from the more natural article of fuel, *coal*, led us to experiment in this direction, with the result of several years ago abolishing our manure-beds and depending entirely upon our FIRE HOT-BEDS for producing winter headed lettuce and vegetable plants for early spring use. Indeed, our labors in this direction have given us such unbounded satisfaction, and we find that the use of such structures is so illy understood by the gardeners of our country, that we will proceed to describe a fire hot-bed in its simplest form, such a one as may be constructed by any farmer or gardener of ordinary intelligence entirely with his own hands, the only outlay necessary more than in the construction of a common manure-bed being for brick of which to build the furnace, and the pipes for constructing the flue. The bed should be built on ground having a natural rise of about one foot in twenty, at least. We have constructed them with a rise of one foot in every ten, in length of bed, for fifty feet, and then turned at a right angle and run twenty-five feet with scarcely any rise at all, the flue terminating in a wooden chimney twelve feet high, and with no trouble for draught. The warmest part of such a bed is at the angle, fifty feet from the fire, as the heat readily ascends to that point. It will be understood that these beds differ but little in appearance from a common manure-bed. A trench is exca-vated six feet in width, about two feet in depth, and of any desired length, say from twenty-five to seventy-five feet, or perhaps even longer, though we believe that to be sufficient for one fire. At the lower end of this excavation the

furnace is built, in the simplest manner, of
brick; and the fire and heat flue, through
which the draught and smoke pass, runs up
through the centre of the trench. Stakes, made
of 3 by 4-inch scantling, are driven along the
sides of the trench at intervals of eight feet,
and it is then boarded up on the inside of the
stakes to a height of three feet on the north or
back side, and two and one-half on the front,
which should be the south side, in order that it
may lie to the sun and be sheltered from the
north winds. The cross sleepers for the floor
should now be placed. Near the furnace, where
the pipes get very hot, the floor should be at
least twelve inches above the pipes, but after
getting twenty feet from the furnace it may be
gradually lowered to within two or three inches,
care being taken to keep the distance great
enough to permit a free circulation of air over
the pipes. Above the floor we are to have
space for six inches or more of soil, and eight
to sixteen inches between the soil and glass for
growth of plants. More than this amount
will be found unnecessary, and, in fact, damaging, as the whole structure should be kept as
low as possible, in order to economize warmth.
The spaces between the side boarding and earth

at the sides of the trench should be entirely
filled with dry forest-leaves or some other good
non-conductor. Common 3 by 6 feet sashes
are used crosswise of the bed, precisely as on a
manure-bed. Perhaps the only part that needs
further description is the furnace. Ours have
been constructed, in the simplest manner, of
common brick, but, of course, fire-brick would
be more lasting. The height of the fireplace
is two feet, ten inches of this being below the
grate-bars for an ash-pit, and fourteen above
the grate for fire. The width necessary for the
fireplace of a bed of the above size is twelve
inches.

The grate-bars are each cast separately, and
are about thirty inches in length, which form
the depth of the furnace from front to rear.
Eight of these bars are required, each occupying a space of one and a half inches. Immediately back of the furnace there should be
a rise of six or eight inches, to prevent ashes
and cinders from being drawn up into the pipes.
The best article for pipes is the common terra-
cotta, which is manufactured and used extensively as a substitute for brick chimneys in
dwellings. We have found it necessary to con-
struct the first ten feet of the flue of brick, as

the sudden heating of the pipes, so near the furnace, is quite sure to crack them.   Common drain-tile may be safely used at a little distance from the fire, and is cheaper than terra-cotta ware.   The pipes, of whatever construction, should be at least six inches in inside diameter. Good terra-cotta pipes of this size can be purchased in our vicinity at about twenty-five cents per running foot, and in this item consists the main cost of this kind of a bed over a common manure-bed.   Of fuel, we have the advantage over many sections of country, in being near enough the anthracite-coal region to enable us to procure a supply at very small cost.   We have, however, found one ton of chestnut coal amply sufficient to run a bed seventy-five feet in length for six weeks, and there are few sections of country in which the cost of coal is so great as to compare with the value of a sufficient quantity of horse manure, capable of producing the same amount of heat. When using manure for a bed of this size, we found that, to produce a good and lasting heat, at least one wagon-load for each 3 by 6 sash was required.   This would cost here at least $2 per load, which, for the twenty-five sashes required to cover the seventy-five feet of bed, would amount to $50, which is much more than the cost of constructing the furnace-bed, including cost of pipes.

So we contend that a bed of this construction is cheaper, even for the first year of use, than the common manure-beds ; while, in after years, when manure-beds have to be refilled entirely, at as great cost as at first, the fire-beds are ready to start any day desired, at no cost whatever. Of course, the spent manure taken from a hot-bed can be used for fertilizing the soil, but in most instances it is so fire-fanged and burned out as to be of comparatively little value.

The time and care required in attending a fire-bed is no more than in those of the common construction. A fierce, hot fire is not required. In moderate weather we have found it necessary to replenish the fuel but two or three times per day, a slow and gentle, but long-continued development of heat being all that is required. For the purpose of keeping a good supply of warm water for watering the growing plants, we place a large pan or kettle over the fireplace.

As it will not do to use cold water, which would chill and injure the plants, early in the season, the importance of having this supply of warm water at hand will readily be appreciated. This furnace is covered or enclosed by a small building, which should be shut off by a partition from the plant-beds beyond, as but little heat is developed in the furnace-room. If the steam from the heating water can be conducted into the beds, its presence will be desirable, as the fire heat has a tendency to dry out the beds rapidly, and this tendency is overcome by the moisture from the condensing steam. It is well, also, to keep a small dish of water standing on the heat-pipe, the arising vapors from which serve the same purpose.

In sections where coal cannot be obtained cheaply enough to enable the gardener to make use of a ton for this purpose, hard wood may, of course, be substituted, with the single disadvantage of the additional time and care thus entailed upon attending the fire.

One great advantage, of which we have not yet spoken, that the fire-bed has over a manure-bed, is the ease with which the temperature may be regulated to conform to the ever-changing external temperature.

When a sudden cold snap, with its howling north winds, comes down upon the manager of the manure-beds, his only hope of escape is to closely cover all his beds with blanket and mat, for it is beyond his power to increase the intensity of the heat ; but with the fire-bed, how different ! All that is necessary, on all ordinary occasions, is to increase the fire upon the evening of the coldest nights. Indeed, we have found the use of straw mats almost unnecessary, if the sashes fit as closely as they should, and the sides are properly banked and filled with dry leaves to prevent the escape of heat.

Cost of Sash.—Good 3 by 6 hot-bed sash, glazed and painted, ready for use, can now be bought at Binghamton, N. Y., at $2.25 each. This is the most expensive item in the construction of any ho.-bed, but it is an expense that cannot well be avoided. Various substitutes have been devised for the glass, but, so far as we have experimented, without avail.

Good Cotton Sheeting will sometimes answer a very good purpose for late use, after the danger of very cold weather has passed ; but its use is attended with considerable annoyance, and, although cheaper in the beginning, it has, with us, proved more expensive in the end, as it will last but very few years.

SHUTTERS.—If glass sashes cannot be afforded in sufficient quantity to cover the desired area, we prefer light basswood shutters to the use of cloth. These are made exactly the size of the sashes in use, and are alternated with them, care being taken to change the position every day, so the glass will cover the space which was covered on the previous day by the shutter, that no part of the bed will suffer for want of light. These shutters will be found very useful in covering the glass frames on cold nights, and also in shading them during intensely sunny weather.

USE OF FLATS.—We have used both a solid floor in the bottom of the bed, on which the soil is placed to a depth of six or eight inches, and movable " flats," which are best and cheapest made of soap or saleratus boxes sawed in two pieces. When these are used, no other floor is necessary, only a series of cross sleepers on which to rest the edges of the boxes. For some kinds of plants there is much gained in the use of such boxes, as they enable the operator to readily shift the growing plants to a cooler or hotter position in the bed, as may be required. These " flats" are also desirable when selling early plants in the market, as they remain fresh and vigorous for several days, and need not have the roots disturbed, until sold to the planter.

SMALLER BOXES.— The latest device for safety in transplanting is the use of small boxes, but three or four inches square, and without bottom. They are formed of four pieces of thin wood, dovetailed together after the manner of the well-known Crandall's Building Blocks for Children. These boxes fit closely together, and a single plant is transplanted into each box. When ready to plant out in the garden, the sides are taken off and the soil placed in the ground without in the least disturbing the roots. These blocks occupy but little room when packed away, and answer the desired purpose very nicely. They are the invention of Mr. Crandall, and are sold through his general agents, the Orange Judd Company, of New York, and can probably be supplied by most seedsmen in retail quantities.

In most sections of this country it will pay the gardener well to grow a crop of head-lettuce in his beds during winter. Even two crops may be grown, but the ground cannot well be cleared in spring in time for starting a good supply of cabbage and tomato plants after the second.

EARLY-CABBAGE SEEDS will be the first to be sown in hot-beds in spring, especially if none are wintered over in cold frames, and north of the latitude of New York, as a general rule, it is considered more risky and troublesome to winter them over than to grow them in hot-beds in spring. The seeds are generally sown about the middle of February.

NEVER SOW BROADCAST, but always in drills about four inches apart, and thinly enough so the plants will not crowd each other and grow spindling. It seems hardly necessary to urge the importance of selecting the very best *quality* of seeds obtainable. If the seeds are in any way inferior, all the labor of planting and attending the crop, with its attendant risks, is lost. Indeed, we can think of no parallel case in which a supposed saving may result in greater loss and waste than in sowing seeds which you have the slightest idea may be inferior, if those above suspicion can be obtained at any price. Still this rule should not be so rigidly adhered to as to suppose that the dealer or grower who charges the greatest price must necessarily have the best article, for competition has brought the price of nearly all seeds very low at present.

COVERING.—Cabbage seed should be covered from one-fourth to one-half inch in depth, and to insure its rapid germination the surface soil should be *firmed*, or pressed down, so as to lie compactly around the seeds.

VARIETIES.—There are so many varieties of early cabbage to be found in the various catalogues, that the planter of but little experience is quite at a loss to know which to select. Yet among them all there are a few so far above the majority in actual worth, that we will speak only of what we consider the very best. For earliest use, the *Early Jersey Wakefield* is still regarded as the standard. *Henderson's Early Summer*, though not quite as early as the Wakefield, is so far ahead of it in size that most gardeners who have tested it now prefer to await the difference in time, as it is by far the *largest very early cabbage grown*.

True, there are varieties earlier than the Wakefield, and some may differ with us in classing it as earliest. The Early York and others are undoubtedly earlier, but as they are at their best a mere handful of leaves, we can see no pleasure or profit in growing them.

Next in order of ripening to Henderson's Summer comes the well-known *Early Winnigstadt*, and closely following this the *Fottler's Early Drumhead*, which, for a general-purpose cabbage, we consider the *best the world has yet seen.* There may be other early varieties which have more merit than these four, but if there are such, we have not yet seen them. We have a field of cabbage this season containing forty-five early and late varieties. A report of their comparative merits may be found in the latter pages of this work.

Soil for Hot-Beds.—A great mistake made by many novices in gardening is to use soil in hot-beds which is *too heavy*, so that the frequent waterings pack it down tightly, and the hot sun bakes it so hard that nothing can grow in it as it ought. The soil for this purpose should be much lighter and looser than common garden soil usually is.

How to obtain it.—When working manure-beds, it was our usual custom to throw out the dirt each summer as soon as through with the beds for the season, and shovel out with the soil a large portion of the underlying manure. This mixture was left in a conical pile which was covered up with fresh stable manure in the fall, which kept the frost out, and allowed it to decompose and decay sufficiently to become fine, loose mould by spring. It can be manufactured in a similar manner for use in the fire-beds. Sandy soil and manure are placed in alternate layers, and built up into a conical pile which is left for one year. Then, when cut down and mixed over thoroughly, it is in an admirable condition for use. If it is thought necessary to use a fertilizer in the beds, we have generally found it the safest and best course to apply it in a liquid form by mixing a little hen manure, or guano in the water with which they are sprinkled. If the soil has plenty of well-rotted manure in its composition, there is usually but little use of further enriching it.

CONSIDERABLE CAUTION is necessary about applying strong fertilizers, or special manures, such as phosphates, guano, etc., to the surface of the beds. The area is so small, and the desire to have the work well done so strong, that it is frequently overdone to such an extent that the germs are killed outright before they see daylight, and then the seller of the seeds is lucky if he does not have to shoulder the blame and receive the charge of selling stale seeds.

TEMPERATURE.—Every hot-bed should have one or more thermometers for showing at all times the temperature of the bed, for it is necessary to the health of the plants that it does not vary too much.   Considerable variation is allowable.   The mercury may run from time to time from 50° to 80° as extremes, though the mean, which is 65°, should be as closely kept as possible.

AIR AND LIGHT.—The influence of light and air is fully as necessary to healthy plant-growth as it is to animals.   If kept from the light and air, a plant grows pale and spindling ; still it is at all times necessary to guard against too sudden an admission of air of a different temperature from that within, as such a change, or perhaps a continuance of a very warm and wet atmosphere, with an occasional admission of cold air, tends to produce what is known as

" DAMPING OFF" of the plants.   This is a shrivelling or wasting away of the body of the plant just above the surface of the ground un-

til but a mere thread is left, which continues
to support the plant with considerable vitality
for some time, but finally effects its ruin.
This disease is seldom seen, however, except
among plants which have grown too rapidly
for their own good and have been at times
kept too warm.

WATERING.—Although the covering of glass
holds the moisture from escaping as vapor to a
considerable extent, the shallowness of the soil
will not enable it to hold water for a great
length of time during sunny weather, and the
beds have to receive an artificial watering frequently. The best time to perform this work
is about four o'clock in the afternoon.

PUMPS.—The nicest manner of accomplishing this is by use of a small force-pump and
sprinkler, which latter is but a small thumb-
nozzle on the end of a short hose, through
which the water is thrown after being drawn
by the pump from a pail. The pump known
as Page's does good work, but is constructed
of tin, and is consequently not very durable.
One manufactured by W. & B. Douglas, Mid-
dletown, Ct., which retails at $9, is the best
and most durable article of this kind we have
yet seen. The great advantage these have over

the more common method of sprinkling with a watering-pot is in doing away with the necessity of removing the sash at each operation. With the pump, the sash has only to be raised a few inches in front and the end of the hose introduced, to give the whole surface a complete wetting with a fine spray.

CAULIFLOWER AND CELERY PLANTS require about the same temperature and general treatment as cabbage. Beds containing these plants should be kept rather cool, say below 60°.

TOMATO, PEPPER, AND EGG PLANTS should never be kept in the same beds with the cabbage, but partitions should separate them, so that the tomatoes, etc., can be kept 15° or 20° warmer than cabbage.

LETTUCE should be classed with cabbage and all other *hardy* plants as regards the proper temperature, while most flowering plants are about *half-hardy*, and require about the same as tomatoes. The main crop of celery plants is generally planted out in open ground ; but for early use a few may be planted to advantage along the front side of the bed where it is partly shaded, as celery revels in a *moist*, half-shady situation.

SOWING FINE SEEDS is an operation in which

a little ignorance frequently leads to much dis-
appointment. By fine seeds we mean such as
celery and the seeds of various flowering plants,
which are so very small that, if covered with
soil to any considerable depth, they will not
germinate ; and on the other hand, if left on
the surface, they will soon become too dry to
sprout. Hence many failures are made, and
the seeds are frequently suspected of lacking
vitality, when the fault really lies in the bad
manner in which they were planted. Such
seeds should be sown upon fresh, moist soil,
and little or no covering, save, perhaps, a slight
brushing of the surface, given them. The
proper conditions for stimulating vitality must
be brought about by properly *firming*, or press-
ing the surface soil around the seed, and a
proper degree of *moisture* and *light* must be
kept until the plant has taken root. One of
the best modes of accomplishing these ends is
to sow the seeds in slight depressions, or drills,
then brush a very slight amount of soil over
them, water the surface well with a fine spray,
and then cover it by laying directly upon the
soil a pane of glass or a piece of cotton sheeting. It must then be watched, and this covering left only until the seeds have sprouted and

the first little root started downwards. The coverings are then removed, frequent but small waterings given, and, if the weather is sunny, a partial shade placed over the beds to prevent the tender plants being scorched in their earliest infancy.

TRANSPLANTING.—This is one of the most important of all hot-bed operations. An abundance of good, fine, fibrous roots cannot be obtained without several times transplanting the young plants. Different species of plants are, of course, benefited to a different degree by this operation. For instance, the cabbage and kindred plants only require room to develop roots and grow in a natural, short, and stocky form ; hence only one removal from the crowded seed-bed to new quarters, where they are two or three inches distant from each other, is all they require to produce good plants, while tomatoes and other plants of similar habits throw out new roots readily, wherever the stem is covered with soil ; hence, if frequently removed, and each time not only given more room to spread, but each time set deeper in the soil than formerly, an astonishing amount of fibrous roots may be obtained, and the more numerous the fibres in proportion to the amount of top, the more valuable is a plant considered when ready to plant out in its final stand in the field. For these reasons, in order to produce strictly first-class tomato plants, it is considered necessary that they be transplanted two or three times before being offered for sale or planted out.

To do this work correctly and rapidly is no mean accomplishment, for it will not bear slighting. Here is one of the advantages of having the young plants in *flats*, as above described, as they can be taken out of the beds, placed upon a table, and the operator allowed to sit in a natural position while transplanting into other flats or boxes which are put in a suitable place in the bed. Where these are not used, but a solid floor, covered by a continuous bed of dirt, instead, the transplanting becomes a more laborious business; but this method has one advantage, at least, in its favor; that is, a greater depth of soil can be used than can be handled readily in flats, hence less watering, and less liability to dry out rapidly when not closely watched. In transplanting in a permanent or immovable bed, the operator lies upon his breast on a wide board which spans the bed crosswise. A thin strip of siding, a little less in length than the width of the bed, is sharpened to an edge on one of its sides. This is forced into the soil to the depth the plants are expected to require; a row of plants is then placed in this groove, at a proper distance apart, and the soil placed firmly against them. Care must be taken that they are placed straight or upright; for if laid over horizontally, they must necessarily grow crooked. The distance apart will depend upon the size of the plant and length of time it is expected to remain before another removal.

Assorting.—Before pricking them out in this manner, it is always well to assort the plants, placing those of equal size together, otherwise the more vigorous will overreach and crowd the weaker ones to their permanent injury. As soon as the bed is filled, a copious watering should be given and the bed shaded for a day or more. The shutters previously described are very useful for shading; and late in the season, when the sun's rays become powerful under the glasses, it is frequently found necessary to cover the glass with a thick coating of common lime whitewash.

Mice, both the common house species and

also the meadow mouse, and the white-bellied, jumping, or woods mouse, are very apt to take up their abode in a hot-bed, the warmth affording a very agreeable protection to them at this season of the year. They are sure to manifest their presence by digging up the seeds which the gardener has sown and burrowing in the soil among the plants. The safest remedy we know, is to set a good trap for them at the time of making the bed, so as to greet them upon first arrival. If allowed to get possession in any considerable numbers, poisoning will probably have to be resorted to.

COLD FRAMES.—The final transplanting of hot-bed plants, previous to their being placed in the field, should consist of a removal into cold frames, which are externally the same as hot-beds, but differ from them in not being supplied with artificial bottom heat, the glass sashes giving them all the protection necessary ; and after they have become accustomed to the new quarters, the covering is dispensed with by degrees, and the plants are thus " hardened off," so that their growth may not be suddenly checked when planted out in the open field.

SWEET-POTATO PLANTS.—The sweet potato is not extensively raised north of forty degrees north latitude; still by setting good strong plants of the earliest varieties, by the first of June, on rich, sandy ridges, fair crops of good tubers may be obtained for home use, and the demand for plants is sufficient to warrant a dealer in vegetable plants in keeping at least a few thousand in supply. There are growers no farther south than central Ohio who make the production of sweet-potato plants almost a sole business, and annually sell hundreds of thousands of them. North of this latitude, the variety which has given the greatest satisfaction in the past is the Early Nansemond. This variety has been kept for years in northern Ohio, where the sweet potato is profitably grown, although at quite a high latitude. It has therefore become acclimated, and will probably do better at the north when planted from these northern-grown tubes than if the seed was brought from the south. A new variety has lately been introduced, called the *Early Peabody*, which is claimed to be at least ten days earlier than the Nansemond, while at the same time it grows larger and is of excellent quality. If, upon further trial, all these claims are sustained, it certainly will prove a very valuable acquisition to northern planters.

For raising plants, medium or small-sized tubers are usually selected. As they require a high temperature and dry atmosphere to keep well over winter, it is difficult to succeed in keeping them sound without having all the appliances for making a special business of it, and keeping in large quantities. The proper temperature for successfully keeping them is from fifty to sixty-five degrees. If exposed to a temperature of only forty degrees, they will be liable to rot, especially if not perfectly dry.

On these accounts it is generally found the best policy for northern growers who want but a few bushels to purchase them, when wanted in spring, of some one who makes a specialty of keeping them. Mr. W. W. Rathbone, of Marietta, Ohio, is in this business, and seed from him will do well in every respect at the north.

The large potatoes to be found in our city markets every fall and spring are not fit for seed for northern planting, for two reasons: first, they are too large and contain too few eyes; and secondly, they are usually of late varieties which can only be matured at the south. It takes about four weeks' time after bedding the potatoes in spring to get the first crop of plants, or sets; consequently, if they are to be sprouted in manure-beds, calculations must be made to get the bed in good working order, and ready to bed the tubers by the middle of April. This will bring the first crop of plants by the middle of May and the second crop by the first of June. The first crop can then be pulled off and transplanted in another bed, where they will continue to grow so as to be stout and well rooted by first of June. There is little if ánything to be gained in setting them out in the field before that time, as the soil must be warm for them to grow. The forcing-bed is made of a layer of about three inches of a light, sandy loam, which is improved by mixing with it a quantity of light leaf-mould. On this the potatoes are laid thickly in rows side by side. Those over one inch in diameter are cut in two lengthwise, and laid with cut side up. The bedding must be done during a warm sunny afternoon, for, as we have said, they are easily chilled, and more easily injured than would be supposed. They are covered with one and a half or two inches of the same material which underlies them. If this soil can be mixed with coal-dust, dry black muck, or even buckwheat hulls, it will help to loosen it, and, in addition, the sun's rays will to a greater extent be absorbed on account of the dark color of the surface, and the bed consequently be made warmer. It is not necessary to cover these beds entirely with glass. The shutters, already described, may be made to do good service here, and the amount of glass at command made to go twice as far. The plants should not be pulled until they are quite well rooted, and if they can then be transplanted into another bed for a couple of weeks, they will be greatly improved, though few of the sweet-potato plants offered for sale are transplanted. Care must be exercised in pulling, or separating the plant from the tuber, not to displace the tuber or break off the sprouts which may have started for a second crop.

As this work may fall into the hands of many readers who may desire to try growing a few sweet potatoes at the north, a few words on the subject of setting the plants, and the treatment of them, though hardly within the scope of the work, may not be entirely out of place. Never lose sight of the fact that the sweet potato is, by nature, a semi-tropical plant; therefore everything you can do to increase the warmth of the soil in which it is grown should be done.

When the plants are ready, and the season far enough advanced for setting them, do not wait for a rain, but proceed with the work. *Never* think of setting them on level—that is, unridged—ground, but after thoroughly ploughing and manuring the soil, ridge it up in high, narrow ridges. A gravelly loam is best, and, as we have said of the soil for the propagating beds, if it can be mixed with coal-dust, black muck, or some other *loosening, dark-colored* material, which will not only enliven the soil, but by its *color* absorb more of the sun's rays, it will help matters wonderfully.

The ridges are now slightly levelled off at top, and will be found in fine order for setting the plants, which is easily done by the hand, on the ridges, at the distance of about eighteen inches apart. The rows, or centres of ridges, should be three feet apart, so that horse cultivation can be given. These ridges are not to be worked down in after-cultivation, but left with straight or nearly perpendicular sides, so that the sun can warm them through. If set on the level surface, the vines will grow luxuriantly enough, but will shade the soil and keep it too cool to produce good tubers. With the above system of cultivation, and a selection of early varieties, we believe that the sweet potato is capable of being grown with profit even as far north as central and western New York. A soil containing a large proportion of coarse gravel-stones, with a general tendency to sandiness, we have found far preferable for growing good specimens of sweet potatoes to one whose base is clay.

PART SECOND.

PLANTS IN THE OPEN GROUND.

CABBAGE PLANTS.—One of the most difficult and vexing parts of all garden operations
is to secure a good supply of healthy, growing
plants. Indeed, after this feat is accomplished,
if the soil is sufficiently enriched, in the right
mechanical condition, and the proper cultivation given, there is little left for a man to do
but to harvest a bountiful crop.

Nine tenths of the failures in this branch of
business are directly assignable to some mis-
management in the first stages of the plants'
growth, and as in all animal nature, a disease or
injury contracted in infancy, though perhaps
for a long time latent, may finally develop into
complete ruin. The general ignorance which
exists throughout this country on the subject
of insects and diseases from which the cabbage
is liable to destruction, may be inferred when

we state that our sales of cabbage plants to market gardeners and planters have ranged to upwards of eight hundred thousand in a single spring. Nearly all the purchasers of these, at least all those who bought in large quantities, would have grown their own plants, had they been satisfied that they could have produced as good and healthy plants at home as they received from us. In some seasons (the present, 1877, being a remarkable one in this respect) every thing will be so favorable that in many localities plants in abundance can be grown by mere chance, nothing happening to attack them to their detriment. But this chance cannot be depended upon safely, for in a majority of instances it will simply result in failure. In how many thousands of instances does a man's experience culminate somewhat as follows:

A man desires to raise a field of cabbage. He first consults all the seed catalogues and works on gardening in his possession, to acquaint himself with the best varieties for his particular purpose. Having made his selection, he dispatches a dollar or two to some seedsman of his acquaintance, for his supply of fresh seeds. He now begins to see difficulties looming up in the distance. He knows by past experience that if he sows the seeds upon the open ground, an arch-enemy awaits the coming of the tender plants, in the shape of a small *flea-beetle.* There are several varieties of this insect, the most destructive to cabbage, and in fact to all the *Brassica* family, being the *Haltica Striolata,* or striped-backed flea-beetle, whose ravages, if not suppressed at once, will finally end with complete destruction to the plant. He therefore follows a time-honored, but senseless, custom, and seeks to escape this enemy by building a seed-bed up a few feet from the ground, *on stilts,* as it were, and by constant watchfulness, coupled with frequent applications of lime and plaster-dust, he partially succeeds; and although his plants are badly spotted by the " little bugs," he keeps them alive, and by frequent waterings causes them to make a spindling growth until nearly large enough to transplant. Of course he boasts of his success, and upon the first rainy day prepares for the transplanting into his field. But what is his dismay upon pulling the first handful to find, instead of the nice fibrous roots seen in his imagination, and which he knows should exist on healthy plants, but *one long, straight tap-root*, which for moisture has run down to the very bottom of the bed, and perhaps already terminates in a ball of fungous growth, which shows that the dreaded "club-root" is already asserting its claims! Upon a closer inspection, he finds the fibres have been eaten off by a *small white maggot*, numbers of which can be found burrowing into the remaining root, and maiming it until it can scarcely be made to live at all. There is but one wise and safe course left for him to follow—which is, to condemn the whole lot, and depend for his supply of plants upon purchasing of some one who understands the management of these difficulties and is glad to take advantage of these misfortunes to increase his own profits by selling him well-grown, healthy plants.

This picture is not overdrawn. Hundreds of men have come to us to rehearse the substance of the above, evidently thinking such troubles were unknown to us, as we always had a supply of plants which had an abundance of roots, and proved to remain healthy when transported to other grounds. Indeed, from the many failures which are continually being reported to us in this direction, we have come to believe that not more than one half the cabbage seeds sold in this country ever produce plants which live to become of sufficient size for setting in the field. The main crop of cabbage is produced from plants which are set during June and July, and at this hot season of the year it is with considerable difficulty that plants can be conveyed by express long distances, even with packing carefully ; and the carrier's charges are so high, that on purchased plants the first cost is frequently doubled or even trebled by the time they reach the planter.

Knowing all these difficulties, we hope and trust that every purchaser of this work will be abundantly satisfied by our showing him how to overcome and remedy them, inasmuch as we do it at the risk of decreasing our own plant trade. Now, in order to come at this subject understandingly to our readers, we shall have to follow it up in a sort of backward way, after stating that the three evils above pictured—viz., *Club-root*, *White Maggot*, and *Flea-beetle—are dependent upon each other, in the order named, for their own existence.*

CLUB-ROOT is an unnatural enlargement, of a spongy or fungoid character, of the root of the plant. It is not confined to the cabbage, but is frequently developed in cauliflowers, turnips, and indeed in all the members of the *Brassica* or cabbage family. So far as our knowledge extends, there is no *cure* for this malady ; for after it makes its appearance upon a plant, it increases in size until it so seriously affects the circulation of the sap, that the plant wilts, turns yellow, and finally dies—a slow death, but one as sure as that of an animal on which a vampire has settled and sucked its life-blood away. But we believe there is a *prevention*, which is infinitely better than the best of cures, for a cure must be preceded by an attack of the disease, which cannot take place without injury. So far as our extended observations have shown, the enlargement called *club-root* is primarily caused by the root being mutilated by an insect. There may be different insects capable of bringing about the same result, if each burrow into and mutilate the root in the same manner and to the same extent ; but allowing this to be the case, it will readily be admitted that the one that is the most common cause, the one that is culpable in the main, is the one which most seriously engages our attention. This we believe to be none other than

THE CABBAGE MAGGOT.—This is the same little miscreant which we have already alluded to, which gets into the plant-beds and eats the fibrous roots off the growing plants, leaving only the one tap-root, which, in order to make a desperate effort to sustain the plant alone, runs down two or three times its natural length, and, if it be fortunate enough to escape the fungoid *Club-root, may* put out new fibres from its sides, after being removed from the vicinity of its parasitic enemies, the maggots. But the *chances* are against it; the *Fates* have thrown their arms around it, and, in the majority of instances, its future course is downward, its doom is sealed.

"Well," once exclaimed a well-informed market-gardener, who is certainly a closer reasoner upon most subjects than the habits of insects, "when your soil gets as full of those little white worms as mine is, you will have to stop growing cabbage plants." And, indeed, he is not the only man who has fallen into the error of supposing, or taking it for granted, that because these worms make their appearance in his plant-beds that they previously existed in his soil as naturally as "angle-worms," and that to escape their ravages he must find some spot where they are not in the soil, or "burn them out" by building a large fire upon the spot to be occupied! Misguided mortal! Does he forget that "where the carrion is there will the ravens be"? that it is Nature's law to place her subjects, great or small, where the food and surroundings are congenial to them? Is it not easier to suppose that these little worms or maggots are bred upon the roots of the plant which is most suitable to their life and purposes? Such we find to be the case, not merely in theory, but in proven *fact*.

This brings us to the question, From whence do they come?—a question easily answered. Why a question so easily solved should remain so long in the dark, or why an answer so easily suspected should escape a single observing mortal, we cannot conjecture; but such has been the case. Can the reader think of many instances in which any species of maggots are reproductive in themselves? In other words, does a worm lay an egg to produce a worm? Such is not the rule in the insect world.

There are three phases to most insect life. First, the *perfect insect*, which is generally a winged insect—a fly, a bug, a beetle, or a miller or moth.   This knows by instinct an appropriate place to nourish its young, and *only* in such places does it lay its eggs. The eggs hatch and bring forth worms, or maggots. The honey-bee lays hers within the cells of her hive, and her subjects go forth into the fields and gather nectar for their sustenance. The skipper-fly selects for her breeding ground the crevices of a rich old cheese, and depends upon its strength and substance for support. Should *either* lack the God-given instinct which enables it to select a congenial spot, its species would become extinct.

We are now ready for the information that the parent of our little *cabbage maggot* is none other than one to whom we have already been introduced, the STRIPED FLEA-BEETLE. Therefore, if we would escape the *maggot*, and through it the *club-root*, we must, from the beginning, *keep our plants free from the attacks of these voracious plant-eaters, the striped flea-beetles*. They are very destructive to the young plants of the cabbage family, are known by various names, such as *turnip-fly*, *radish-fly*, etc., but more properly as *Haltica Striolata*, or *flea-beetle*.

There are two species very common in this

country, one being entirely black and one having two bright golden or yellow stripes upon his back. Their habits are similar. When approached they will spring from the plant in a true flea-like manner, and, if in imagined danger, feign inanimation in a 'possum-like manner. This trait of their character may readily be taken advantage of by cooping in the vicinity of the beds a hen which has a good brood of chickens old enough to run freely among the plants. The chicks soon learn the trick, and make a reality of the feint of death by relentlessly swallowing all of them which come within their reach; and as by constantly running amongst the plants they continually scare them off, we have never discovered a better remedy for beds already infested with them than this; and were the simple eating of the plants the extent of the mischief of which they are capable, this remedy, with perhaps an occasional sprinkling of plaster, carbolic powder, soot, or any thing distasteful or injurious to them, would be all the remedy to be desired. But as we have shown that the amount they *eat* is nothing in comparison to the damage following the laying of their eggs, with the attendant results, you will at once see the importance of keeping the seed leaves *unspotted* by their greedy jaws. In order to accomplish this, it is necessary to consider that the maggot, after becoming full-grown, changes into the pupa state, and remains in the ground for about two weeks, when it again comes forth to continue its depredations upon the plant, which by this time has grown so large as not to be seriously injured by being slightly eaten. So they continue to infest plants of the cabbage family until fall; and the last litter for the season remaining dormant in the pupa state over winter, come forth perfect beetles during the first warm days of spring, ready to attack the first tender plants which appear.

Our Preventive will now be readily understood by every careful reader. By knowing where these pests are to abound—which is wherever there was a quantity of cabbage, turnips, radishes, mustard, or any plant which they infest, growing during the preceding summer and fall—*there* in early spring may we look for the fleas, *and as far from there as possible must we sow our cabbage and kindred seeds.* But the insects have wings, and will they not go to our beds as soon as the plants are up?

This is just what we must prevent them from doing—a task more easily accomplished than may be imagined. We know almost the exact spot from which they will come out of the ground, so our first care must be to provide food for them and keep them there. For this purpose we sow, on the ground which was occupied the previous summer with cabbage and turnips, as early in spring as possible, a mixture of cabbage, turnip, and mustard seeds. These may be any old, mixed, or doubtful seeds, which are always accumulating, and are of no particular value. Cheap imported cabbage seeds will here answer an excellent purpose, as their only use is for *bug food*, and after serving their purpose, are to be ploughed under before they breed a second crop. Of course, we must expect an instalment of bugs or fleas from our neighbors' grounds, if we do not prevent their coming in some way.

By sowing our seeds, as we have shown, upon soil and in a vicinity not occupied the previous season by any vegetation of the kind, we have to contend with no fleas except those which come from other quarters. Let us now inquire what causes them to come, or how they are enabled to find our young plants.

Nature has furnished them with but one mode of accomplishing this, and that is by the sense of smell. It then follows, that if we in some manner *destroy* or *change* the natural smell of the young plants which we wish to protect, no further trouble will result. This must be done by creating some *other* smell powerful enough to overcome the scent of the cabbage plant. There are several ways of accomplishing this. Turpentine, mixed with dry plaster, and sprinkled upon the plants as soon as they come up, and repeated as often as it ceases to send out its peculiar scent, will often effectually keep them away. Coal-tar, which can be bought at the gas-works for $2.50 per barrel, has a very strong, disagreeable smell, and is probably as cheap as any thing which will answer this purpose. It is not necessary to put it directly on the plants. If a few quarts are spread upon boards and placed in the immediate vicinity of the young plants it will completely hide the scent of the cabbage, and but an occasional chance bug will find them, especially if the bugs are furnished with an abundance of food elsewhere, as described above. Remember, the idea is not to let them come on the plants, and then try to drive them off by applying something distasteful to them ; but apply the remedy even before the plants are up, to screen them so they will never be found. In addition to these precautions, every thing possible should be done in the way of preparing the seed-bed, and using fertilizers that will cause the plants to come up stout and healthy, with large, green seed-leaves, and keep them in condition to grow as rapidly as possible, so the third leaf may come out before a bug shall find them.

After the third leaf has made its appearance there is generally but little danger of an attack, especially if there is a supply of younger plants provided for them in the neighborhood. The first, or seed-leaves, of the cabbage are all the bugs seem to have any special liking for. They will, however, usually hang to a mustard plant nearly all summer, so we usually sow a good-sized patch of the white or French mustard for their special benefit. We frequently use the same ground for raising plants two or more years in succession, and find that if we clear every trace of cabbage from it as soon as the plant season is over, but few bugs will be found in the vicinity the following spring.

As these assertions are at variance with the

writings of other authors who have written
upon these subjects, our readers may desire to
know what proof we can present to sustain
them. Well, these are the principles upon
which we have worked for the past ten years,
during which time we have grown, annually,
hundreds of thousands of plants. Never, during all this time, have we seen a single case of
club-root developed upon a plant which had
not first been mutilated in its roots by the cabbage maggot, and never have we discovered a
trace of the maggot in the roots of plants
which had not first been severely worked upon
by the flea-beetles.

On the other hand, never have we had a
bed of plants severely attacked by the beetles
or fleas that was not subsequently injured by
the maggot ; and further, never have we yet
seen a maggot in the root, or the slightest tendency towards the development of club-root,
on a plant, or plot of plants, which had been
absolutely protected from the flea-beetles.
Although strong, this of course is only circum-
stantial evidence. We have taken a lot of
these maggots from a bed badly infested with
them, put them into a glass cage, and kept
them until they developed into perfect little

flea-beetles, which is as strong proof as we are now able to present. The closest observers agree that *club-root* is caused by a little worm boring into the root. Why not, then, as soon lay the mischief to this little maggot as any other, inasmuch as it is more frequently found here than any other worm. We do not doubt but that there are other maggots, the larvæ of other insects than the flea-beetle, which are capable of producing the same effect, but we do believe this to be the most common cause and the one most to be guarded against. We are aware that altogether a different code of habits has been given these insects by prominent entomologists and writers upon this subject, and desire to quote a few passages, that the reader may be led to experiment until satisfied who is right. Hon. Asa Fitch, in his "Eleventh Report of the Noxious, Beneficial and other Insects of the State of New York," which was published in the Twenty-sixth Annual Report of the State Agricultural Society, in writing of the cabbage maggot makes the following statement :

" It lies dormant in the ground about a fortnight in its pupa state, and then gives out the perfect insect, which is a two-winged fly *resem-*

bling the common house-fly, but somewhat smaller in size, measuring 0.20 in length to the end of its body and 0.26 to the tip of the closed wings. . . . . This cabbage fly is so closely related to the onion fly, that the same remarks made respecting the remedies for that species will apply equally well to this." In speaking of the *striped flea-beetle*, in the same Report, he describes certain " crooked marks" to be seen upon the *leaves* of cabbage and turnip plants, and says : " These marks are really produced by minute worms living in the interior of the leaves, feeding upon their green pulpy substance, and leaving the skin unbroken, mining a serpentine track, which increases in thickness as the worm grows to a larger size. These worms are the larvæ of the flea-beetles, which make most of these marks, which occur in the turnip and other leaves in the garden."

It is but justice to state that this fallacy— for we have proved it to be such—did not originate with Mr. Fitch, but is credited as being a new and valuable discovery, made by a Mr. Le Keux, a member of the Entomological Society of London. But Mr. Fitch heartily endorses it, and so it has been handed down and accepted as a truth among the entomological fraternity. We think the error has continued long enough for the good of the cabbage, turnip, and radish growers of our country, so we have given our own opinions freely upon the subject, and will await the decisions of careful experimenters as to the correctness of our views.

THE RADISH MAGGOT.—Mr. Fitch, in the Report above alluded to, lays the parentage of this well-known worm to a different fly from the one which he thinks produces the cabbage maggot. In our opinion—which is founded upon practice and careful observations—it is *the same*, neither being the product of a " fly resembling a house-fly," but both emanating from the eggs of the striped flea-beetle. We do not say that there is no other fly in existence whose eggs produce worms which feed upon the roots of either cabbage or radish. There may be such an insect, but we have never seen it. We write only of what we know, not of what may exist beyond our knowledge. Our experience has been with radishes the same as with cabbages.

Whenever we have kept the young radish plants entirely free from the ravages of the fleas, and had them on loose, rich ground, where they could grow rapidly, we have invariably had splendid tender radishes, without a trace of worms; but when the young plants were badly eaten by the fleas, we always found worms in the roots—unless it might be with early varieties, whose growth was forced so rapidly that the worms had not time to show themselves before the radishes were pulled. We have said that this insect winters in the pupa state—meaning that they usually do so; but we think the perfect insects also frequently live through the winter in a dormant state, as they make their appearance very early in the spring.

The same methods given for protecting cabbage plants will apply to radishes with equal force. Where but a small bed of plants is to be grown, a method probably as cheap, and of as little trouble as any, will be to sow early, and protect the bed a great part of the time, while the plants are young, with a covering of glass sash or cloth. But it will be found vastly more difficult to raise a small bed of plants and keep them healthy and free from insects, than to grow them on a large scale. It will also be found cheaper for a man who wants but a few hundred or thousand cabbage plants to purchase them of some one who grows them largely, than to attempt to grow his own. During the season just passed, we furnished our customers who came to the beds with as fine, healthy, well-rooted plants as they could desire, and of the best varieties, at $1.50 per thousand. Who could think of preparing his bed, purchasing his seed, and producing a single thousand for that money?

If it be found impossible to keep the fleas entirely off, on account of neglecting some of the precautions which we have given, the best manner of overcoming the injuries likely to be developed is to keep the plants growing as thriftily as possible, from the time the seed leaves are opened until the head is formed, as it frequently happens that where the plants are not *badly* infested with fleas, the diseases resulting therefrom will be comparatively slight.

THE USE OF LIME upon ground occupied by cabbage is commonly regarded as beneficial, many growers having noticed that club-root is less likely to be developed where lime is a plentiful constituent of the soil. The reason for this is obvious: the strong alkali is very destructive to the maggots, and keeps them in check.   Wood ashes are, for the same reason, one of the best fertilizers for all this class of plants.   Beautiful turnips and radishes may be grown on a newly cleared fallow with scarcely a trace of the maggot.   The great amount of potash contained in the ashes is supposed to be their most valuable element for this use, as this class of plants, and in fact all leguminous plants, require a great amount of potash.

Aside from its alkaline nature, lime has, in our opinion, but little manurial value *in itself.* Of course some of its constituents enter into the structure of the plant, but its main use or value as a manurial element consists in its action upon the vegetable matter with which it comes in contact, its tendency being to decompose or set free the gases bound up in the vegetable tissue, and render them available as plant food.   Therefore, when lime is used in combination with vegetable manure or with animal excrement, the mixture should always be kept under cover of the soil, that the gases may be held from escaping until the plant absorbs them.

PLASTER OR GYPSUM is in its effects exactly opposite to lime.   It has a great affinity for ammonia, phosphoric acid, and potash, and readily absorbs them, especially the former, from the atmosphere, or from any thing containing these gases with which it may chance to come in contact. Plaster, but no lime, should therefore be placed in all composts or mixtures which are to be used as surface manures. The kind of land most likely to be benefited by lime is therefore that which already contains a large amount of muck, or any vegetable matter. Our best market-gardeners generally apply lime to their grounds the year following a heavy application of stable manure, the first crop being fed by the parts of the manure which are readily soluble, and the lime serving to decompose the residue for the second year's use.

SPECIAL OR COMMERCIAL FERTILIZERS.— This is a subject which is commanding a great amount of thought and attention of late. There being few localities where an abundance of stable manure can be obtained, the importance of finding a substitute is apparent. The three principal elements required by the majority of our farm and garden crops, and which are not already to be found in sufficient quantities in the soil, are ammonia, potash, and phosphoric acid. Ammonia most largely abounds in all animal substances, all nitrogenous bodies. Potash is largely found in ashes, and is also obtained in large quantities for commercial use from potash-rock, which is mined extensively in Germany, and also in some parts of South Carolina. Phosphoric acid is most readily obtained from bones, and is the most valuable constituent of the various superphosphates and bone manures with which the markets are filled.

The exact proportion of each of these ingredients which is required for perfecting any of our farm or garden crops is readily ascertained by analysis. It seems, therefore, that it would be an easy matter to compound a special fertilizer which should be exactly adapted to any plant or crop. And this course is strongly advocated by many eminent agriculturists at the present day. We have not in practice gone farther in this direction than to compound these elements into a fertilizer which we have used upon a general line of field and garden crops. The use of such a fertilizer has been attended with varying results upon the different crops, some being particularly gratifying.

The largest mixture of this kind which we have yet used, we will give, not as a pattern for others to follow, but to furnish an idea of the substances and proportions which we deemed necessary in a special or general fertilizer. First we obtained one ton of fine dry *hen manure*, this, at $20 per ton, being our cheapest source of ammonia. Next, one ton of *muriate of potash*, at $50. Third, one ton of fine *dissolved bone*, at $35. These three substances were finely compounded, and mixed with three tons of *gypsum* or *plaster*. One or two barrels of this mixture per acre, sowed upon wheat in early spring, gave, upon a piece of old land, where oats the previous year were scarcely worth harvesting, the most bountiful yield we ever grew. Twice that quantity sowed upon a piece of ground which had not received a coating of stable manure in fifteen years, gave us as rank a growth of cabbage plants as we desire to see. We seldom venture the experiment of putting such manures in the hill, but always prefer sowing broadcast, and lightly harrowing in.

But users of these concentrated commercial fertilizers must not for a moment think that they are going to entirely take the place or perform the functions of stable manure. They will not. The amount of soluble plant food contained in a load of stable manure is by no means the extent of its value. The mechanical action, the loosening and lightening influence which the vegetable matter has upon our stiff clay soils particularly, is of the greatest importance. The strongest commercial fertilizer in the world, on a stiff, heavy clay soil, destitute of vegetable matter, will give very meagre returns. Ploughing under clover and other green crops must then be resorted to in connection with special manures, in order to make their use satisfactory to the planter.

PREPARING GROUND FOR CABBAGE PLANTS. —From what we have written, the reader will understand the reason for our now saying, select for your cabbage seeds a spot as far distant from where they have been previously grown as possible. There is scarcely any possible preparation, for either a field of cabbage or a bed of growing plants, better than ploughing under a good heavy growth of large clover the previous summer. The clover always leaves the ground in a loose, light, mellow, healthy condition for the following spring's work, so that comparatively little stable manure will be required. If it is desired to sow the cabbage seeds early in spring, we usually plough the ground thoroughly and leave it in ridges the fall previous, so that it will more readily dry off and become in good working order in spring. Then, as soon in the spring as it is in fit condition, it is ploughed and harrowed down finely, and furrowed out in beds about three and a half feet wide. The beds are then raked down, or rather the stones and lumps raked out into the furrows, which leaves the ground very nearly level again. There should, if possible, be ditches enough left so that the water from sudden rains may be carried off, otherwise the beds may suffer from washing during the frequent rains which come at this season. Whatever special manure we are to apply may be sown upon the surface and harrowed in before the beds are furrowed out, or, if the quantity is limited and we desire to make it go as far as possible, it may be sown upon the beds after the first raking, which is usually done with a four-tined potato-digging hook. It is then raked again with a steel-toothed rake, care being taken to rake the small stones and lumps to the surface by a movement of the rake lengthwise of the bed, so as not to rake the fertilizer into the ditch, but to thoroughly mix it with the surface soil.

The bed is then ready for sowing the seeds, which is readily accomplished with a common

onion or turnip seed-drill. We have used both
Matthews' and Comstock's seed-drills, and
think the former the best instrument for sowing seeds simply, and the latter the best we
know of that has a cultivator attachment.
These machines will sow any kind of seeds,
from mustard up to corn and peas, with much
more regularity than can be done by hand, at
the same time with much greater rapidity, and
with an exactness that allows any given number of pounds of seeds per acre to be sown.
They cost from $8 to $12 each, and can be procured through any seedsman. With these machines the seeds are sown in drills lengthwise
of the beds, four rows being placed upon each
bed. This brings the rows about ten inches
apart, with a space of one foot between each
two beds, which is used as a path.

Cabbage seeds require but little heat to
germinate freely, and, if the weather is favorable, they should begin to show themselves in
one week. We have frequently had cold
weather, and even snow, after our earliest sowing was up, but never have had them injured
by it. We make our first sowings as soon in
spring as we can get the ground in suitable
condition, which is not until from the 12th to

25th of April with us. We then continue to sow at intervals of one week until the 1st of June, at which date our first out-doors plants are ready for sale or transplanting. We have dwelt sufficiently upon the importance as well as the manner of keeping the young plants protected from insects. To accomplish this will require constant watchfulness, and no one should undertake the job who has not the necessary time to enable him to outgeneral his small but powerful enemy.

CULTIVATION.—The soil around the young plants should be frequently stirred, both for the purpose of stimulating their growth and destroying all weeds which make their appearance.

The best hoe we have ever found for this purpose is easily made by taking a piece of inch-wide hoop-iron, say thirteen inches in length, and grinding one of its edges quite sharp. Now punch a couple of holes through each end, or one half inch from each end, large enough to hold a shingle-nail or a three-quarter-inch screw. Next find an old hoe-handle, or make one out of a cast-off rake's tail, and fasten the end of it securely into a hole in the centre of a hardwood block five inches in length, making it T-shaped. Now bend the hoop-iron at right angles in two places, four inches from each end, making it ⊔-shaped, and fit it upon the cross-piece on the handle, fastening it with screws or nails, which pass through the holes near the ends of the hoop-iron, and into the ends of the cross-piece. Fasten it at such an angle that when the hoe-handle is held in the hands in a natural position for hoeing, the ⊔ will stand upright. Now, as this hoe is drawn along between the rows of cabbage, it cuts and kills every weed, and loosens the soil without displacing it, as it simply passes through the loop and falls back into position. This also makes a very superior onion weeder. Of course the dimensions given—five inches, which makes the width of the hoe—can be varied at pleasure, but should be somewhat less than the distance between the rows where it is expected to be used.

TRANSPLANTING.—A cloudy or wet time is usually selected for transplanting the plants into the field; but if they are good, tough, healthy, well-rooted plants, and the soil contains the usual amount of moisture, as good " luck " may be had in pleasant weather as during a rain. The ground should be worked up fine and mellow by thorough ploughing and harrowing. We usually set by stakes; one person dropping the plants on the line, and another following and setting them with a " dibber," which is a sharp stick, eight inches long, for making the hole into which the plant is dropped to the right depth. They may be expected to wilt some; but, if the soil is loose and moist, not one per cent. will die from transplanting, and they will commence growing sooner, while the ground will be left in far better condition than it will be after setting in, or immediately after a heavy rain, as is frequently done. The striped flea-beetle sometimes attacks early cabbage plants after they are set in the field. Should they do so, it is proof that they have nothing more suitable to eat, and should at once be furnished by sowing seeds of turnip, mustard, etc., in the immediate vicinity, at the same time dusting the plants with plaster or wood ashes. The fleas should, however, be kept from finding the young cabbage plants in the manner so fully described under head of Striped Flea-beetle, and our prevention.

VARIETIES.—There are so many varieties of cabbage in cultivation, that the inexperienced planter is frequently at a loss to know which to select. It is easy for us to enumerate those which usually give the best satisfaction in our soil and climate, but this information might be no criterion for people in other localities.

Under the head of Early Varieties, in Part First of this work, we stated that we valued *Fottler's Early Drumhead* above every other variety for a general-purpose cabbage. We will also place it at the head of our list of late varieties; for, although called early, if planted late—say from 25th of June to 10th of July in this latitude—we have yet to see its equal for fall and winter use. It has a large, hard, flat, and beautifully shaped head, which is always formed on a short stem. It is very reliable for heading, and has probably grown more rapidly in public favor during the past few years, in this vicinity at least, than any other variety. In order to ascertain what it would do in other localities, we made an offer last fall to send a sample package of the seeds free to any cabbage-grower who would give it a trial and report results. The offer was published in several popular agricultural journals, and in response we received nearly five hundred applications. Nearly every State and Territory in the Union was included in the list, and we are pleased to state that, so far as received, the reports speak very favorably of it.

THE FLAT DUTCH, in its different strains, is by far more widely and extensively cultivated throughout this country than any other variety. Nearly every seed-grower has a particular strain of this variety which he claims to be superior to any to be obtained elsewhere. The truth is there is little difference in them, and any one which has been for years selected for seed purposes, and only those which have formed perfect heads saved and planted for producing seeds, will give satisfaction. English-grown seeds of late varieties of cabbage usually fail entirely to produce good heads in this country, and should never be planted with the expectation of obtaining more than a good growth of leaves for fodder. We attribute as a reason for this, not that the climate is unfavorable, for it is even better or more perfectly adapted to the wants of the cabbage than our own, but to the fact that these imported seeds are usually very carelessly grown from stumps, refuse heads, or plants which have failed to head at all. The reason for importing these seeds is that they can be procured for less money than American-grown seeds. So a *cheap* article is produced to meet the demand, but in the end it is found to be the dearest. If seed stock from some of our standard varieties should be taken to Europe and there carefully developed, then the finest heads selected and seeds again grown from them and brought back to our country, we believe they would produce even finer heads than the original cabbages here. We base these conclusions upon similar experiments which we have made by sending to Washington Territory, where the climate, in the vicinity of Puget Sound, more nearly resembles that of England than our Middle States. Still we believe that if propagated in these warm and moist lacalities for a long series of years, the tendency would be to ripen later and later each succeeding year, until they would become unfitted for our short seasons, as it is a well-known fact that vegetables of any kind will ripen sooner when the seeds are procured from far north than south of the locality in which they are planted.

French grown cabbage seeds seem to do much better with us than English, but as American seeds are superior to either and can

now be produced at a cost low enough to sat-
isfy any one, there no longer remains even this
poor excuse for importing.

The *Late Drumhead* is quite a popular late
variety. It is later than the *Flat Dutch*, and
usually not so reliable for heading.

We this season planted forty-five early and
late varieties, in order to ascertain if there were
any better than those of which we have
spoken. A casual observer would not suspect
that the field contained more than a half dozen
varieties. Among the early varieties, the *Little
Pixie*, *Early Wyman*, *Cannon-ball*, *Early
Flat Dutch*, and *Schweinfurth Quintal*, ap-
peared to possess more real merit than any
others, except those named on pages 19 and
20. The above rank in earliness and size
about in the order named. The *Little Pixie*
is earlier even than the old *Early York*. The
heads are small, but very hard. An admirable
first early variety. The *Early Wyman* somewhat resembles the *Wakefield*. It grows
rather larger, and may perhaps be an improvement on that well-known variety. The *Cannon-ball* produces what its name indicates, a
very hard, round head, probably harder than
any other variety.

The *Schweinfurth Quintal* is very reliable for heading. The heads are uniformly large, the largest in the field, but are not very solid. They are of fine shape, white, tender, and of excellent quality.

The *Early Dark Red Erfurt* is an improvement on the old *Red Dutch*. It is earlier, of a deeper color, grows on a shorter stem, and produces a fair-sized, very hard head.

The *Bergen Drumhead* seems to be earlier than the common *Late Drumhead*, and much more reliable for heading.

The *Stone Mason* seems of late somewhat prone to rot in the stem before ripening. Otherwise it is an excellent second early variety. Several other varieties might be considered valuable but for their liability to destruction by rotting. Among these we would name *Wheeler's Imperial*, *Robinson's Champion*, *Fearnaught*, and *Filderkraut*. The last named, but for this fault, would be a very excellent variety. It somewhat resembles the *Winnigstadt* in shape and habits of growth, but is even more pointed than that justly popular variety. The *Silverleaf Drumhead*, *French Quintal*, *Green Glazed*, *Dax Drumhead*, imported *Flat Brunswick Drumhead*, and *Enfield Market* failed entirely to produce heads of any value in our trial patch. Although we ought not to approve or condemn any variety on a single trial, we feel justifiable in recommending those which produced fine heads as preferable to those which made entire failures, as they had in all respects an equal chance. The *Improved American Savoy* is probably the best of its class. The savoys are the tenderest and finest in quality of all cabbages. The heads do not usually grow very large or very solid. They are more especially grown for family use, where fine quality is more of an object than quantity.

THE CUT-WORM is the next enemy which stands ready to claim the plants. It is so old an offender, and so well known, that no description is necessary. We regret that we know of no manner of exterminating them cheaply and effectually. If very plentiful, they may be seen while preparing the ground, and if the planter has no other spot well adapted to cabbage which is not so badly infested with them, he must either lose a large percentage of his plants, rid the ground of the pests before setting them, or so prepare them that they cannot be eaten off by the worms.

His peculiar circumstances must enable him to
decide which of these three alternatives is his
best hold.

The plants may be easily prepared to withstand this enemy by wrapping each stem with
a small strip of thin paper, which, when the
plant is set in position, will extend down to, or
slightly into, the soil, and up one or two inches
from the surface. There are, doubtless, prepa-
rations in which the stems of the plants may
be dipped which will also repel or kill the
worm, and still not injure the plant. Experiments in this direction might result in valuable discoveries.

If a few days' time can be spared between
preparing the ground and setting the plants,
these worms may be pretty effectually extermi-
nated by sowing a quantity of beans over the
piece and lightly harrowing or raking them in.
They will come up quickly and be attacked by
the cut-worms. Then, by passing over the
ground daily for a few days and hunting the
worms, which are readily found just under the
surface, close by the plants which they have
just cut down, the patch can readily be cleared
of the pests.

THE GREEN WORM.—The next enemy from

whose depredations the cabbage is likely to suffer is the white cabbage butterfly, which has been in this country but a few years, and is the parent of the much detested green cabbage worm. For a year or two after its advent in this country it caused general and almost complete destruction. Now it injures the plants to some extent, but by no means so severely as formerly. The reason for this is that its natural enemies have also become numerous enough to keep it in check. Like all other insects, there are three stages to its existence—viz., the perfect insect, which is the butterfly ; the caterpillar, or green worm, in which form it is most destructive ; and third, the *chrysalis*, or pupa state, in which it is dormant, and undergoes the change from worm to butterfly. When in this state, and to all appearances lifeless, in which condition it passes the winter, it is sought by a small parasitic fly, which punctures its skin and lays within its shell a number of small eggs. These soon hatch out into little white maggots, which eat the inside entirely out, leaving only a hollow shell. We have examined dozens of these chrysalides in early spring—which are to be found on the sides of buildings, fences, stones, or any rubbish near

where cabbage was grown the year previous—
without finding a single one not infected and
spoiled by these maggots. So much reduced
has this cabbage pest become by means of this
parasite, that if all the worms found while hoeing the plants are carefully destroyed, little
damage will be done to large plantations, even
if no more attention is paid to them. Where
but a few plants are set-out in the garden, however, the damage will be proportionately much
greater, and if not frequently destroyed, the
worms may effect a complete ruin.

The reason for this is, that the butterflies,
which lay the eggs, are very active insects, being
almost continually on the wing, and wandering
around from field to field. Wherever they can
find cabbage they stop and lay a few eggs, and
pass on. The consequence is that the eggs,
and soon after the resulting worms, become
nearly as numerous on the small patch as upon
the large, and of course, if there are more
worms in proportion to the number of cabbages, the resulting damage will be correspond-
ingly greater. The butterflies are attracted to
the cabbage by the sense of smell, and may in
a great measure be prevented from finding
them in the same manner as we have describ-

ed for the prevention of the flea-beetle. As this *prevention* is vastly better than any *cure* with which we are acquainted, we will not occupy space by giving *remedies*, especially as we know no infallible one.

SALTING CABBAGE.—An application of a few bushels of salt per acre, sown upon the soil when preparing it for cabbage, is very beneficial, the cabbage being naturally a salt-water plant, or one which grows to its greatest perfection on lands contiguous to the sea-shore. Salt also has a good effect in destroying worms upon any soil, and may be used very beneficially upon any lands infested with white grubs or cut worms.

An article well adapted to these purposes is the refuse or dirty salt, which may frequently be obtained at the salt-works at from $2 to $5 per ton. It must not be used too freely, however, or the results will be attended with more loss than profit. We have in mind an instance in which we procured four barrels of refuse salt, which we intended to apply as a top-dressing on nearly as many acres, mainly for the purpose of drawing or holding the moisture during the dry summer months. The work of applying was left to a man who misunderstood the matter entirely, and the contents of the four barrels were spread, with a shovel, upon about one third of an acre in the centre of a field which we afterwards planted with potatoes. The result, as any one might naturally infer, was a total dearth of vegetation upon that land for one year. Not even a weed dared to lift its head, and a casual observer might have supposed that a pond of water had recently dried away, leaving the middle of our field clean and bare. The following season that spot was selected as a site for carrots and asparagus plants, both of which grew finely, and with but little trouble from weeds.

Judging from the results of this experiment, we believe that a heavy application of salt might frequently be made to pay upon rich, old grounds which have become badly infested with weeds, though at a loss of use for one season. A small pinch of salt sprinkled upon the heads of growing cabbage is also thought to cause them to grow larger and more solid. It may be repeated at intervals of one or two weeks, each time enlarging the quantity. Care must be exercised, however, not to overdo this work, as too large a dose would result disastrously.

WATERING THE PLANTS IN THE SEED-BED.
—It is commonly supposed that young growing plants require very frequent watering during dry seasons. Whether this supposition is correct or not depends entirely upon the condition of the plants. If they are healthy, with leaves unspotted by bugs, and abundantly supplied with fibrous roots, they are capable of withstanding as severe drought as any other class of plants. But if maimed and crippled in both leaf and root, as is too frequently the case when grown by parties who know not how to take care of them, the hot sun and withering winds will curl them to such an extent that frequent watering is the only means of sustaining life.

CELERY PLANTS.

THE consumption of this delicious vegetable is greatly on the increase in this country. This causes the demand for celery plants to annually become larger, and as there is considerable knack in producing a good lot of plants, it has become an important branch of business with many seedsmen and vegetable gardeners.

It is useless to attempt to grow a bed of

celery plants on our sunny sidehills in the open ground. If forced to produce them in such situations, it must be done in frames, where they can be easily watered and partially shaded. The natural situation for celery seems to be in a moist, cool, half-shady position, near a body of water, whose vapors as they continually arise will give the atmosphere a perceptible feeling of dampness. A rich, mucky or loamy soil is best adapted to the needs of this plant.

As a spot eminently fitted in these respects is usually very slow to dry out, it will generally be found too wet to get in order and sow as early in spring as it is necessary the seeds should be sown in order to produce large, stocky plants, in time to fully develop during our short seasons. We would, therefore, recommend working the soil up in good condition during the dry fall months previous, and leaving it in high ridges over winter. All that is necessary in spring will be to rake down the beds as early as the weather will permit, and sow the seeds.

The seeds should always be sown in drills, as directed for cabbage plants, about ten inches apart, but may be considerably thicker in the rows than cabbage. They must not, however, be covered as deeply as cabbage seeds. The manner of sowing usually decides the crop. If properly done, they will come up evenly and produce a good crop of plants; but if improperly done, the chances of an even catch are slim.

The seeds must be covered but very lightly, a mere sprinkling, enough to hide them from sight, being sufficient. Then, to prevent their drying out, the soil must be "firmed." The simplest manner of doing this on a small scale is to pack the soil on the rows with the feet. Walk over each row twice, by placing one foot as closely ahead of the other as possible, so that your whole weight will press upon every inch of the row. Beds so treated will come up evenly, when if this simple firming was omitted only here and there a plant could be seen.

Celery seeds are slow to germinate at the best. Every thing being favorable, two weeks' time will elapse between the sowing and the first appearance of the plants. For this reason if for no other, the plants should be in rows, and the rows far enough apart, so they can be easily hoed out and the weeds kept in check.

Celery plants, to become large, stocky, and of good shape, should be transplanted, or "pricked out," as gardeners term it, as soon as they have attained a height of two inches, into a bed of rich, mellow soil, in rows four to six inches apart, and two inches in the row.

Here they should receive frequent waterings, and should be sheared or cut back as often as they show any tendency to send up tall and spindling leaf-stalks. This keeps them short and stocky, and causes them to form a mass of fibrous roots. They will then be ready to start into vigorous growth as soon as put out in the field, where they have plenty of room. They may be left in these beds until the removal of some early field or garden crop gives a vacant spot for setting them, and will be growing probably more rapidly in the beds during the hot and dry weeks of midsummer than they would in the field.

ASPARAGUS PLANTS.

ONE of the best paying vegetables for marketing at the present day, if rightly managed, is asparagus. A grower of vegetable plants will therefore find a good demand among his customers for asparagus plants, and as they are very easily grown they may be sold at seemingly low prices, yet at a fair profit.

The requisites for an asparagus plant bed arc a light, rich, sandy loam, *free from weeds.* This latter is an indispensable quality, for the seeds are several weeks in germinating, and if the ground is full of weed-seeds, they will spring up and occupy the land so far in advance of the asparagus, that it can never catch up. Therefore, select a spot which is smooth and level, which has been in potatoes, cabbage, or some hoed crop the previous year, and kept free from weeds. Plough, furrow, and rake it into beds early in spring, as directed for cabbage seeds. Sow the seeds with a drill, three or four rows upon each bed, mixing with it a few radish seeds. These will spring up at once, and thus enable the ground to be hoed or cultivated before the young asparagus plants have made their appearance. All that is now necessary is keeping the weeds from growing, and thinning out the asparagus plants, if too thick, to about three inches apart. If upon good soil and well taken care of, these one-year-old plants will be good for setting in permanent beds in spring. Two-year-old plants are very frequently used, but a first-class one-year-old is considered fully as valuable as one which, on account of neglect, has occupied two years in attaining a suitable size for setting.

Asparagus plants are perfectly hardy, and may be safely wintered in the beds without protection, yet, if upon soil which is liable to heave by frost, a slight covering will prevent damage.

STRAWBERRY PLANTS.

Should you ask persons who grow strawberries if they have any young plants to spare, nine out of ten will say, " Oh, yes ! thousands of them." You go after them, and you will probably find an old bed which has become matted with vines, yet when you undertake to dig them it is with great difficulty that you can obtain a dozen good plants. There may be thousands, but they are so crowded, and have occupied the ground so long, that the majority of them are either too old to be of any value to transplant, or else too weak and small.

Growing plants and growing berries are separate and distinct branches of business, and cannot well be both done at the same time in the same beds. Because a man grows berries, it should not, therefore, be inferred that he has young plants to spare. He may have, or he may not. To produce nice berries, the runners should be kept cut so that the old plant will stool out and become large and thrifty. To produce good plants, they must be allowed to run for one season only, on fresh soil, free from weeds, where the young rootlets can readily take hold. Strawberry plants are fit for setting only during the season in which they are formed, or early in the following spring. If older than this, the roots become hard and black, when it is with difficulty that they can be made to live, and they are not at all likely to grow thriftily. On the other hand, if too young, or grown in old, crowded, or weedy beds, the roots will be few and short, and the plants generally too weak and feeble to do well. The usual method for obtaining plants is to keep the bed in condition for producing fruit for one year. Then remove the mulching and cultivate between the rows thoroughly, letting the runners grow the next season after fruiting.

When we get choice, new varieties, from which we wish to propagate as rapidly as possible, we have found it the best plan to procure them in March, and set at first in a moderate hot-bed, or cold frame, where they will grow rapidly, and usually bloom in April. The blossoms are picked off as soon as formed or while in bud. The next tendency of the plant is to throw out runners, after it has borne or attempted to bear fruit. Early in May, or as soon as all hard frosts are past, we carefully transfer them to the open ground, selecting a situation for them which is free from weeds and weed seeds as possible, and which will be likely to remain somewhat moist at the surface throughout the season. Here they should be placed not nearer than three feet apart each way, and different varieties at least ten feet apart, for they are prepared to throw out run-ners at once, and as they will keep running all the season, until stopped by cold weather late in the fall, the number of plants produced will not only be surprisingly large, but they will be of remarkably fine quality, and well supplied with roots. There is a great difference in the running propensities of different varieties. A hundred plants each of the CAPTAIN JACK and CUMBERLAND TRIUMPH, set out last spring, after the above treatment, have entirely covered the ground with very fine plants; while the GREAT AMERICAN, PROUTY'S SEEDLING and others have shown more of a tendency to stooling, or developing large hills, so that but few plants have been formed.

SETTING THE PLANTS.—Strawberry plants should be taken up carefully with a garden trowel, the roots straightened out, and all decaying leaves and runner stalks neatly trimmed off. It is well also to trim the ends of the roots neatly and smoothly, as new rootlets will readily start out where they are cut. We have somewhat changed our views, during the last few years, in regard to the best manner of setting the plants. We used to accept the plan so frequently recommended, of spreading the roots as much as possible around a small mound on the surface, as the best. But we have found that it will hardly answer in our locality, where we are liable to suffer on account of very dry weather, as the soil is liable to become dry even below the roots, before they have taken a start and the plants die. We therefore have had better success in setting as we would set cabbage plants, by making a hole some three or four inches deep with a dibber, and putting the roots down as far as possible without getting the crown below the surface. This will give the plant moisture until new roots are developed, so that fewer vacancies will be found in the bed.

We believe that nothing is gained in our locality by fall setting, but, on the contrary, spring planting has every thing to recommend it. We know that many claim a half crop the first season upon fall-planted vines. This we have yet to see them do. Of course we get a few, but the extra cost of covering the plants with straw the first winter, which must be removed in order to cultivate in spring, more than balances the gain. In some sections strawberries may be profitably grown without any winter covering, or protection from the cold. But it is not so with us. The continual freezing and thawing lifts the plants from their position little by little, until they are left entirely upon the surface, where the frost and wind hold high carnival over the remains until not a spark of life is left. A winter covering of straw or forest leaves is therefore indispensable, and the cultivator who plants a larger area than he can cover, throws his labor away.

PACKING PLANTS FOR TRANSPORTATION.— If to be sent but a short distance, no particular care will be required in packing, further than to lay them evenly and securely. The roots should be dipped in water in order that they may be kept moist, and the plants retain their freshness ; but the tops must be packed dry. What we must particularly guard against is the liability of the plants to heat, when they will turn yellow and commence to decay rapidly.

We have experimented a great deal on this matter of packing, and will endeavor to describe the method which seems most satisfactory. The plants when pulled are counted out in bunches of one hundred each. After dipping the roots in water, two layers are placed in the box, the roots toward each other. Slightly damp moss is packed on and between the roots to retain moisture there. If to remain packed over twenty-four hours, some perfectly dry hay or straw must be packed in alternate layers with the tops, say one inch of this packing to every three or four inches of plants. In this way the two tiers are built up to the top of the box. A piece of board six inches in width, and as long as the width of the box, is then pressed down upon the roots, and fastened at each end with a nail driven through the sides of the box. The ends of the plants should not come in contact with the box, but a space of at least two inches left for the circulation of air. The sides and top of the box should be composed of slats, also for the free admission of air.

For short distances, we usually take any cheap box of suitable size, place a layer of moss in the bottom, and stand the plants upright in it, packing a sufficient quantity of moss or hay between or around them to hold them in position, and ship with no covering whatever over the top. The express agents and others handling the box will then see at a glance that if they turn the box over the contents will be spilled. The result is, the box is carried right side up, with care. This would hardly do, however, for long distances or in crowded cars. If the box is covered at all, the plants must be securely fastened so they will not shake around whenever the box changes position, as it must be expected to carry with any side up that may happen during the journey.

Second-hand soap and saleratus boxes are of good size and shape for packing-boxes. With the best of packing, plants will not safely withstand more than three days' journey, and a distance occupying two days will be as great as will be found profitable, taking into consideration the risk and also the increased express charges.

We have recently adopted cheap willow baskets for packing but a few hundred plants. They are light, neat, cheap, and admit air freely, so as to carry plants in the best possible condition.

CARE ON ARRIVAL.—Fully as important as that the plants be properly packed, is it that the receiver understand what to do with them when received. The plants will undoubtedly be somewhat wilted and the roots more or less dry. The boxes should be opened as soon as possible upon receipt, the bunches taken out, and the roots dipped in water. The plants should then be laid loosely in some cool, shady place, until they revive and freshen up. Many planters dip the roots in water, and then in dry plaster, before setting out in the field. This helps to retain the moisture to some extent, but if the soil is loose, fresh, and moist, as it should be, but a small percentage of loss will occur. If the plants are much wilted, or the weather so dry or hot that they are likely to wilt badly after setting, all the larger leaves should be removed from the plants, as they will then be much more likely to live.

GROWING SQUASHES.

THE ultimate success or failure of a squash crop depends perhaps as greatly upon the treatment which the plants receive during the first stages of their existence, as that of any vegetable of which we have spoken. We will therefore add a few brief notes on their culture.

A dish of winter squash is so greatly relished by the majority of people, that we wonder they are not considered as staple as potatoes, and a good supply laid in by every family. Unquestionably the best varieties, which have been thoroughly tested in divers localities, are the pure *Hubbard* and *Marblehead*. The *Butman*, a more recent introduction, claims to surpass the above in some points, but is not yet well enough known to be classed as a standard

Either of the above will keep well till spring, providing you have enough so that the cook will leave a few until then. Squashes require a light, dry, rich soil. Do not depend upon a half-bushel of rich soil in the hill, thinking that will give them sustenance sufficient to enable them to run over poor ground. You will never try that plan but once. It will not be successful, for this reason: not only are the main roots very long, but the vine does not depend entirely upon them for its support. At every joint where the vine branches out, a new root strikes down for nutriment.

The squash is a rank feeder, and requires heavy manuring to enable it to perfect its crop between frosts. It is therefore a safe rule to apply at least one half of the allotment of manure broadcast, and one half in the hill.

Our seasons are seldom long enough to enable them to perfect their growth. It is therefore desirable to plant earlier than the late frosts in spring will allow without protection. One of the cheapest and most satisfactory plans we have seen for accomplishing this, is to take a block not over eight or ten inches in diameter, place it on the hill over the seeds after planting, and with a hoe draw the earth around it to a height of four or five inches, packing it as tightly as possible. The block, or mould should be a little larger at the top than at the bottom, so that it may be readily drawn out, leaving the soil in position. The concave thus formed is now covered by laying a pane of glass over it. This concentrates the sun's rays, shelters the hill from cold winds, and protects the plants from frosts and insects. The covering may be left until the plants press against the glasses, when they are removed, and the plants thinned and hoed. If the glasses are thought too expensive, a good quality of paper or piece of cheap muslin fastened down at the corners will answer a very good purpose. Two plants in each hill are better than more, but as they are easily destroyed, the thinning should be left until you are confident that no further loss will occur.

The greatest enemy to the squash vine are "bugs." The large brown bug, so well known as a "stink bug," will devour them more rapidly than any other, yet as the damage done by them consists mainly in the amount they eat, a little watchfulness will save the vines from them.

The yellow and black striped cucumber bug

are the most to be feared, for not only do they damage by the amount they eat, but just so sure as allowed to remain for any considerable time upon the vines, they will literally lay the eggs for the future destruction of whatever escapes their greedy jaws! Therefore banish them entirely. Do not think that, because there are not enough to destroy your plants, they will do no harm. The eggs of these bugs soon hatch into white worms, grubs, or borers, as they are generally termed, which enter the body and main roots of the plants, frequently boring and tunnelling through them until but a resemblance of a honey-comb is left. Then the plant withers and dies. There is no other hope for it. The only remedy is to keep off the bugs. The plans and preventives given elsewhere for saving cabbage plants from the attacks of the flea-beetle, will also apply to squashes with equal force.

Squashes will mix badly if different varieties are planted near each other, or near gourds, or any plants of the same natural order, but the mixture will not show the first season, so it will do no harm, providing the seeds from such specimens are not saved for future planting.

THE POTATO.

NOTES ON THE NEWER VARIETIES.

PROBABLY no vegetable in the catalogues is of greater importance, the world over, than the potato. Therefore, any hints by which the grower may be enabled to improve his crop, in yield or quality, must be regarded as seasonable. Good crops may be grown on a great variety of soils; but a deep, light, sandy loam, or a thoroughly drained peaty soil, is most suitable. A heavy application of stable manure will greatly increase the size of the tubers, and also the general yield; but it will also increase their liability to rot: so that it is not advisable to apply fresh stable manures largely, except in case of early varieties, designed for marketing as soon as dug.

However, we have never yet observed any damaging influence from the use of horse-manure with which plenty of litter has been mixed, and think the loosening properties which such materials have are exactly adapted to the wants of the potato. The best possible position for potatoes is where a light soil has been heavily manured the year previous for some other crop; or, if the soil is somewhat heavy, a good clover sod, plowed under the autumn previous, will make an excellent base on which to grow a heavy crop of potatoes.

The planting should be done early—as soon, in fact, as the soil is in good working order. Our experience has been that, all other things being equal, the earliest planted will yield at least one third more than those which are delayed two or three weeks.

We are convinced that the majority of people plant three times as much seed as they should in order to secure the best results. Probably the average amount used in this country for seed will exceed ten bushels per acre, while the average yield will not exceed one hundred bushels, or at most a ten-fold increase.

Now, we suppose the potato is capable of yielding at the rate of an hundred-fold with common field culture; and by taking a little extra pains, in favorable situations, different parties have succeeded in doing ten times as well as this, even; for upward of one thousand pounds have repeatedly been produced from a single pound of seed.

We have for a number of years practiced

cutting to single eyes; and although we have
never succeeded in obtaining such enormous
yields as those referred to, we find that we get
not only a much larger yield per acre than
formerly, but a far smaller percentage of small-
sized potatoes.

There is no disguising the fact that the potato, when propagated year after year from tubers in the usual manner, is subject to deterio-
ration, degeneration, or a continual " running
out" of its productive capacities. Where are
our " Merinoes," " Mercers," and " Peachblows"
of twenty years ago? Meagre indeed are the
returns from them, compared with what they
were in their youthful days. Our old favorites
cannot be kept. Their day has passed, and
new candidates have taken their places. And
these, in turn, must give way to others as they
become unproductive, as they certainly will in
time.

Our only method of retaining and improving
the productiveness of the potato crop is to
continue to produce new varieties from the
seed-ball. Even the justly celebrated Early
Rose, which at the time of its introduction
was probably without a peer in the world, has
already lost much in this respect, and now has

many superiors. Let it not be supposed that every new seedling is valuable. Men who have produced varieties of especial merit have devoted almost their whole time to the work, and offered to the public only a few of the best from many thousands of seedlings. Who would think of trying to produce from the seed an apple superior to the Northern Spy, Baldwin, or Greening? Yet our finest fruits were once produced from seeds, and the chances of superiority on new potatoes are probably no greater than in the case of fruits. Those who have been most successful have accomplished it by making crosses, or hybridizing the blossoms on the best varieties at their command. In this way great improvements have certainly been made during the past few years, and there is at the present time a list of varieties which we believe more meritorious than was ever offered to the public before—at least, within our recollection. We will append a short description of some which are not yet generally cultivated :

EARLY VARIETIES.—*Alpha.*—This is, without doubt, the earliest variety in cultivation. It is adapted only to garden culture, as the vines are of a very dwarf nature, and it requires rich soil and careful cultivation. Under these conditions a fair crop may be obtained; but with common farm-culture the yield will be very light indeed. It originated with Mr. Pringle, of Vermont.

Early Ohio.—This is, all things considered, the best very early potato we have ever grown. It is of recent introduction. It is a seedling of the Early Rose, and is named after the State in which it originated. It is of nearly the same color as its parent, but differs in shape, being more nearly round. It grows to a large size, is very productive, and of first-rate quality. A decided acquisition.

The Ruby.—This originated with Mr. Pringle of Vermont. It is about with the Early Rose in season of ripening, is of a deeper red color, and is in every way a very desirable variety.

The Snowflake is now so well and favorably known that it scarcely needs description. The tubers present a beautiful, smooth, white appearance, and when properly grown are unsurpassed in quality. It is necessary to seed very lightly with this variety, or it will produce too many small tubers.

Early Vermont very much resembles the Early Rose in every way. We think it is decidedly more productive. At least, it is newer, and consequently more full of vigor.

Carpenter's Seedling.—A long, smooth variety, which has given us much satisfaction. It is an abundant cropper, produces very uniform-sized tubers, of good quality, and is an excellent keeper. Ripens with Early Rose.

LATE VARIETIES.—*Burbank's Seedling* is a beautiful potato of recent introduction, which has few faults and much to recommend it. It is a Massachusetts production. The tubers are long, white, and smooth, somewhat resembling the well-known Prince Albert. Mr. James J. H. Gregory, who has the honor of introducing it, claims for it more desirable points than any potato with which he has experimented for years. In beauty of form it is unexcelled, the proportions being all that can be desired, and is never hollow-hearted. It has the valuable characteristic of yielding almost no small potatoes. Season medium late.

Dunmore Seedling.—This is another valuable new variety of Mr. Gregory's introduction. It is a large, smooth, round, white potato of beautiful appearance, fine quality, and enormous yielding propensities. We have grown many specimens weighing two pounds each, and have not yet seen a hollow one. Its general appearance somewhat resembles the Peerless, but it surpasses that well-known variety in both yield and quality.

The *Calcutta* seedling very closely resembles the Dunmore in every respect. In fact, it is difficult to distinguish single specimens, so close is the resemblance.

The Superior.—This is one of the finest varieties yet introduced by Mr. Brownell, of Vermont. It is a very smooth, long, red potato. Inside it is fine-grained, white, and brittle. It appears to be an excellent keeping variety. As some of Mr. Brownell's former seedlings have been lacking in this essential, it is to be hoped that this variety will remain much longer in public favor than some of them have done.

The *Triumph* is a new variety, recently sent to us from New Hampshire. It is a rather flat, round, or somewhat oblong variety. An abundant cropper, and all that can be desired in quality for table use. It is worthy of a place in every collection. Color, red. Season, medium.

Tioga.—This originated in Genesee County, N. Y. It is of a mottled, red and white color, very smooth and productive, but valued particularly on account of its exceedingly fine quality.

Genesee County King.—Same origin as above. It is a very large, round, free-growing, hearty potato. Its only fault, so far as we can judge, is that the eyes are rather more sunken than is desirable.

The Victor.—A large, smooth, round potato, of a very beautiful light pink or flesh color. It originated in Ohio. 'It seems particularly well adapted to light, sandy soils, and when in just the right situation, has given astonishingly large yields. The quality is somewhat inferior to some of the above varieties, but preferable to many which are more popular than itself.

The *Mahopac* is a seedling of the Early Rose. It is some two weeks later in ripening than its parent, but surpasses it in appearance, yield, and quality.

The above list embraces all the most valuable new varieties which we have thoroughly tested; and we can confidently recommend all or any of them to the public, believing they will give much greater satisfaction than the old, degenerated varieties, to which so many cultivators still tenaciously cling. Experi-

ments have shown us that bringing the seed
from a distance, where it has been grown on
soil of a different character from that on which
it is to be planted, will nearly always cause potatoes to yield far more than where the same
or an equally good variety is continually
propagated on the same soil.

OUR BUSINESS

IS THE PRODUCTION AND SALE OF THE

CHOICEST VARIETIES

OF

Vegetable and Flower Seeds,

VEGETABLE PLANTS,

AND

NEW VARIETIES OF SEED POTATOES.

We invite all who are interested in these things to send us their names and addresses, and we will take pleasure in sending, free, a copy of our latest Priced Catalogue.   Address,

TILLINGHAST BROS.,

Factoryville,

WYOMING CO., PA.

www.ingramcontent.com/pod-product-compliance
Lightning Source LLC
Chambersburg PA
CBHW022343020726
47500CB00004B/1256